Just Not the Same

Addie Lacoe

Illustrated by Pau Estrada

Houghton Mifflin Company

Boston   1992

For Milt and Norah

Library of Congress Cataloging-in-Publication Data

Lacoe, Addie.
    Just not the same / Addie Lacoe ; illustrated by Pau Estrada.
        p.   cm.
    Summary: On their birthday triplets Cleo, Mirabelle, and Gertrude
discover the virtues of compromise and sharing.
    ISBN 0-395-59347-6
    [1. Sharing—Fiction.   2. Triplets—Fiction.   3. Birthdays—
Fiction.]   I. Estrada, Pau, ill.   II. Title.
PZ7.L1356Ju   1992   91-44041
[E]—dc20   CIP
                           AC

Text copyright © 1992 by Addie Lacoe
Illustrations copyright © 1992 by Pau Estrada

Printed in the United States of America

HOR   10   9   8   7   6   5   4   3   2   1

On the first day of October a single, perfect, ripe
apple appeared at the top of the backyard tree.

"I want it," said Cleo.

"No, I want it," said Mirabelle.

"What about me?" said Gertrude. "I want it, too."

Mama cut the apple into three pieces, one for each of them.

"Mirabelle's piece is bigger than mine," said Cleo.

"Gertrude's is bigger than mine," said Mirabelle.

"Mine has a spot on it," said Gertrude.

Mama took back all three pieces and made them into applesauce.

But it was just not the same.

Later that week, the fall leaves were especially colorful.

"Let's all go for a ride in the hills," Daddy said.

"I want to sit up front," said Cleo.

"No, I want to," said Mirabelle.

"What about me?" said Gertrude. "I want to, too."

"You'll have to take turns sitting up front," said Mama.
"There aren't enough seat belts for everybody at once."

"I don't want to wear a seat belt, anyway," said Cleo.

"I want to sit next to the window," said Mirabelle.

"I want to play the radio," said Gertrude.

Mama let all three girls sit up front. And Mama and Daddy sat in the back.

But it was just not the same.

The next day was their birthday, and Daddy bought them
a brand new triple bunk bed, which gave them lots more floor
space to play games or dance or have make-believe tea.

"I want the top bunk," said Cleo.

"No, I want to sleep there," said Mirabelle.

"What about me?" said Gertrude. "I want to sleep on top, too."

"You can't all sleep in one bunk," said Mama. "You're much too big for that."

"I'll have nightmares with somebody sleeping over me," said Cleo.

"I'm putting my favorite poster on the ceiling, where I can look at it," said Mirabelle.

"How are we going to divide the room up if all our beds are on the same spot?" said Gertrude.

Mama and Daddy took the beautiful new bunk bed apart and put all three beds on stilts, each with its own ladder.

But it was just not the same.

That evening Mama called everyone together for a birthday treat. There was so much ice cream that Cleo and Mirabelle and Gertrude weren't even worried about how much they were given.

"All my favorite flavors," said Cleo.

"Would you like sprinkles on top?" asked Mama.

"Yes, please," they all said.

Mama began to count out the sprinkles. "One for Cleo. One for Mirabelle. One for Gertrude."

"You don't have to count them all out," said Mirabelle.

"No, no," said Mama. "They have to be *exactly* equal." She continued counting, "One for Cleo. One for Mirabelle. One for Gertrude."

"Our ice cream's melting," said Gertrude.

"That's all right," said Mama. "It's more important to be absolutely fair." She counted all the more slowly. "One for Cleo. One for Mirabelle. One for Gertrude."

The girls waited and waited for Mama to finish counting the sprinkles. When she was finally done, they ate their ice cream.

But it was just not the same.

Not long after that, their friend Samantha's dog had puppies.

"Samantha said I could have a puppy," said Cleo.

"No, I asked her first," said Mirabelle.

"What about me?" said Gertrude. "I want one, too."

"We can't have *three* puppies," said Mama. "We only have room for one."

"He can sleep in my bed and play with my toys," said Cleo.

"But first I have to feed him and brush him and take him for a walk," said Mirabelle.

"Not until after I dress him up in my doll's clothes and teach him to do tricks," said Gertrude.

"You could have three *toy* dogs, instead," suggested Mama.

"That just wouldn't be the same," said Cleo.

"What about three kittens?" said Mama. "We have room for three little kittens."

"That'd be nice," said Mirabelle, "but it just wouldn't be the same."

"You could all visit the puppy at Samantha's house," said Mama.

"But Samantha can only keep the puppies for one more week," said Gertrude. "And besides, that just wouldn't be the same, either."

The girls thought and thought.

"I hate it when things are just not the same," said Cleo.

"If we shared him, that *really* wouldn't be the same," said Mirabelle.

"We can call him Sprinkles," said Gertrude.

And they did.

And it was just not the same after that.

Just not the same at all.